THE STRANGE ARMADILLO

THE STRANGE ARMADILLO

Wyatt Blassingame

Illustrated with photograp

DODD, MEAD & COMPANY · NEW YORK
A SKYLIGHT BOOK

Photograph Credits

Wyatt Blassingame, 19 (top), 32, 34, 36, 37, 52; Dr. Harry Burchfield, 27, 41; Custom Photographic Labs, 44, 45; Florida Game & Fresh Water Fish Commission, 8; Outdoor Photographers League Photo by Don Shiner, 23; Outdoor Photographers League Photo by Roger Wrenn, 26; © Leonard Lee Rue III, 11, 15, 22; Dr. Eleanor Storrs, 13, 18, 19 (bottom), 33, 53, 54, 56; Texas Parks & Wildlife Department, 14; Linda Ward, 49, 50, 58, 61.

Distributed in Canada by McClelland and Stewart Limited, Toronto
Manufactured in the United States of America

2 3 4 5 6 7 8 9 10

Library of Congress Cataloging in Publication Data

Blassingame, Wyatt.
The strange armadillo.

(A Skylight book)
Includes index.
Summary: Discusses the characteristics and habits of the nine-banded armadillo of the United States and its particular connection to leprosy research. Also presents facts about the nineteen other armadillo species and their cousins, the sloths and the anteaters.
1. Nine-banded armadillo—Juvenile literature.
2. Armadillos—Juvenile literature. [1. Nine-banded armadillo. 2. Armadillos] I. Title.
QL737.E23B56 1983 599.3'1 83-9073
ISBN 0-396-08180-0

For Alice

who should have been with us
chasing armadillos. She'd have
caught one—maybe.

CONTENTS

A nine-banded armadillo

1
THE NINE-BANDED ARMADILLO

The armadillo is a strange animal, in many ways.

It looks strange. It acts strange. And in a strange way it has become very important in the battle against one of mankind's strangest and most terrible diseases.

The armadillo was given its name by the early Spanish explorers in Central America. Since it is native only to the Americas, the Spanish had never seen one before. They must have stared at the first one in great surprise. *El armadillo* they called it, meaning "the little armored one." And it does look somewhat like a soldier's helmet with feet. Or maybe an iron football. But that's only the body. At one end there is a long, round, pointed tail. At the other end is a head almost as long and pointed as the tail. Fully grown, the armadillo may weigh eight to twelve pounds, about the size of a large house cat. Along its back and sides, from its nose to the tip of its tail, it is covered by a stiff, leathery armor. Near the head and rump this armor is solid. But over most of the body it is divided into nine flexible bands. Now and then this number may vary by one or two, but nearly always there are nine bands. A few rough hairs stick out between the bands. Only the belly is unprotected.

Actually there are about twenty species of armadillos, but only one is native to the United States. Scientists call this one *Dasypus novemcinctus*, meaning that it has rough feet and nine bands. Some persons call it the common long-nosed armadillo. Most often it is called the nine-banded armadillo. Later this book will mention other species, but chiefly this is about *Dasypus novemcinctus*.

Hunting for the insects on which it lives, an armadillo moves slowly. If it smells or senses danger in some way, it may stand on its hind feet and appear to be looking and listening. It has big, long-lashed eyes, but it doesn't see well. Its mulelike ears stand straight up, looking too big

If it suspects danger, the armadillo may stand on its hind feet, propping itself up with its tail, to look around.

for its body. But it doesn't hear very well. Its brain is small and when it is hungry it is intent on nothing but food. Moving slowly, it may root right up to the foot of a person standing motionless, watching.

There is a folktale that the best way to catch an armadillo is to decide which way it is going, then get in front of it and stand still. When it bumps into your foot, reach over and pick it up by the tail. This might work, if the armadillo didn't see you move. But if the armadillo did see you, things would happen, fast!

I once set out to catch an armadillo in order to take pictures. My brother, wife, and a friend went with me. None of us thought we'd have any trouble. We'd all seen armadillos rooting alongside the park road, paying no heed to anything. But when we surrounded one and closed in on it, things happened.

A startled armadillo seems to explode. This one leaped straight into the air, twice its own height, legs spraddled. And hit the ground running. It ran straight between my legs before I could bend, ran over my brother's foot, scared my wife into jumping higher than the armadillo

A scientist uses a net of heavy, woven nylon to capture an armadillo in Florida. The armadillo's claws quickly destroy a net of light material. On the other hand, a wire net will seriously cut the armadillo's feet.

had done—and was gone, off the road and into palmettos so thick a snake couldn't have followed.

For an animal that is usually both slow and clumsy, it was amazing. I later learned that for a short distance, the

The jaguarundi, sometimes called the otter cat, lives in southern Texas and Central and South America. It is one of the armadillo's feared enemies.

armadillo can run like a rabbit and outdodge many dogs. But its speed is short-lived. If caught by a large dog or bobcat, the armadillo may curl up slightly, trying to pro-

This is as tight a ball as the nine-banded armadillo can make. Actually it isn't a normal position. The nine-banded armadillo prefers to run, dodge, hide in thick bushes, or dive into a burrow if possible.

tect its soft belly. It cannot, however, roll into a tight ball as many persons believe. The three-banded armadillo of South America can do this, but not the nine-banded.

Nor does the armadillo's armor protect it as well as does the hard shell of a turtle. Its armor is more like tough leather, and can be cut by the teeth of a large animal. The armadillo has teeth, but they are small, far back in the mouth, and no good for biting. It has long claws, but it does not use them for fighting.

Even so, it is the armor and claws on which the armadillo relies for protection. Because of its armor, it can go crashing through briers and brambles that would rip the hide of many animals. Then it tries to find a hole in which to hide. Either smarter than it usually appears, or acting by instinct, the armadillo often has a number of prepared burrows scattered around its hunting area. One armadillo had fifteen within its ten-acre range. And, if necessary, it can usually dig a new one in a hurry.

2
THE ARMADILLO'S HOME AND FOOD

The armadillo's claws are heavy, long, and pointed. There are four on the front feet, five on the back. They could be dangerous weapons. But apparently the armadillo simply doesn't know how to fight. If you pick up an armadillo it may struggle to escape, but it does this by waving its feet in the air rather than striking with them. Any injuries it causes are probably accidental. But because the claws are strong and sharp they can be dangerous. The safest way to pick up a frightened armadillo is by the base of the tail.

When it comes to digging a den with those same claws, the armadillo is a small, high-powered steam shovel. Some persons claim an armadillo can disappear into ground so

Note the powerful claws on both the front and rear feet

hard a man would need a pickax to crack it. That, of course, is not quite true. For one thing, armadillos prefer soft, moist earth where insects are more numerous. Given the kind of ground it wants, the armadillo can create a den that one scientist has described as "an authentic masterpiece of engineering."

The den will have an entrance big enough for the arma-

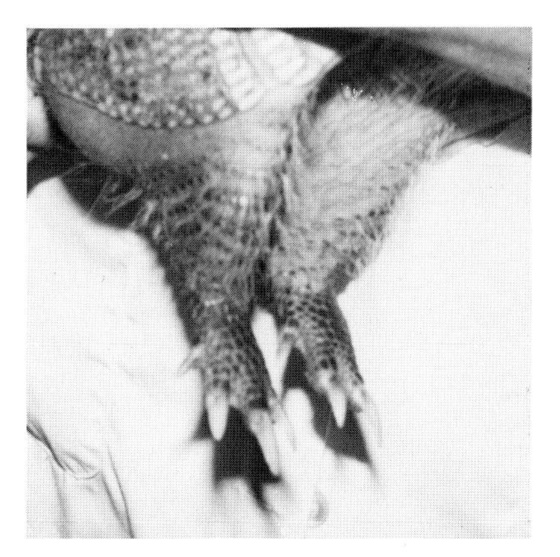

Close up of the back claws on a nine-banded armadillo

A nine-banded armadillo leaving a hole originally dug by a gopher turtle in Florida.

dillo but not much else. The den may run for six feet or more. Quite often it passes beneath the roots of trees that help keep the roof from caving in. At the far end is what might be called the living room, or maybe the bedroom. This is a pit that may be as much as four feet deep. Here the armadillo spends most of its daylight hours, safely asleep.

Normally armadillos tend to be loners and each one has its own den. But they have been known to share a den with a turtle, or rabbit, or even a snake. And if the weather is cold, several armadillos may huddle together in one den.

Farmers sometimes complain about armadillos, saying that horses and cows may step in the dens and break their legs. This does happen, but very rarely. Almost always the armadillo makes its den in a bank or so near the base of a tree or bush that there is little chance a large animal will step in it.

On the other hand, an armadillo can almost destroy a lawn or flower garden in a single night, rooting through it for insects. The insects, left alone, might have done almost as much damage. But it wouldn't have been as sudden, or easily seen.

The armadillo feeds chiefly at night, especially in summer. If hungry it may leave its den in the late afternoon, or on gray, rainy days. But mostly it spends its summer days sleeping. On the other hand, in winter it is much more likely to go hunting for food when the sunlight is warm. The armadillo doesn't like cold. It does not truly hibernate like some animals, but in winter it will spend much of its time curled up in its den to keep warm. In fact, the armadillo's normal body temperature is several degrees below that of most animals. This is one reason it has never spread very far north. It is also the reason the armadillo has become so important in medical research.

Because of its poor eyesight, the armadillo depends chiefly on its senses of touch and smell, whether it hunts by day or night. It roots along like a small pig, its snout buried in the leaves or grass or the soft earth in which it likes to feed. And it eats just about anything eatable that gets in the way. It has been known to eat small snakes. It

A young nine-banded armadillo digging in the soft ground for insects.

eats berries and other vegetation. But chiefly it eats insects. Scientists estimate that one armadillo will eat about 220 pounds of insects each year—and that's a lot of insects.

In feeding, the armadillo uses its tongue. This is surprisingly long, and the armadillo can flick it out and back again as fast as a whiplash. Also the tongue is coated with a kind of thick saliva: each flick may come back covered with insects.

Armadillos like termites and will destroy them by the millions. But they also have a taste for hot foods, or so it seems. The stomachs of armadillos have been found to contain not only fire ants but also scorpions, tarantulas, and spiders. In fact, the stomach of one Mexican armadillo contained ten tarantulas, one scorpion, a snake, and a toad.

Scientists don't know if the thick saliva on the arma-

This massive ant colony, with its ants, eggs, and pupa, would provide a good meal for an armadillo.

dillo's tongue helps to keep it from being stung. But they do know that the armadillo's unarmored belly is not insect-bite proof. At least not completely. Dr. Eleanor Storrs, who has studied armadillos for over twenty years, watched one feeding on fire ants. For several minutes it stood with its long snout buried in the anthill, eating away. Then, suddenly, it jumped back from the anthill. When Dr. Storrs examined the armadillo, there were red spots from ant bites all over its belly. But put on the ground, the armadillo went right back to eating the fire ants.

3
THE ARMADILLO'S FAMILY HISTORY

The ancestors of today's armadillos were roaming around South America some 50 to 55 million years ago. Scientists have classified them in the order Edentata, meaning toothless. Actually, many of them did have teeth, sometimes in large numbers. So now the name Xenarthra is often used rather than Edentata. Anteaters and tree sloths, along with the armadillos, are the only living descendants of this scientific order.

In the time of these ancient Xenarthrans, North and South America were separated by water. But gradually, maybe two or three million years ago, what is now Central America rose up to form a land bridge between North and South America. Over this the armadillos moved

Wearing medieval-looking armor, the nine-banded armadillo has found its way up from South America to Texas, Louisiana, Florida, and even as far north as Missouri and Arkansas. Its armor plate probably accounts for its survival for some 55 million years.

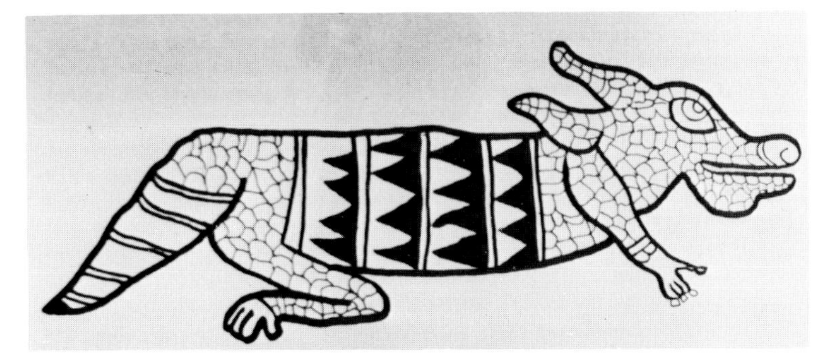

This is a picture of an armadillo painted by an unknown Mayan artist long before the discovery of America by Columbus.

slowly northward. Eventually they were as far north as what it now Missouri and as far east as the Carolinas. Some of those ancient armadillos looked much like the nine-banded armadillos of today. Some were much bigger. At least one species was as big as the black bear.

And then, maybe five or ten thousand years ago, all the armadillos in what is now the United States died out. Why, nobody knows. But in South and Central America the armadillo survived. In Maya legends the black vulture was said to have never died—instead, it changed into an armadillo. Other Indians didn't worry about where the armadillo came from, but they knew it tasted like excellent pork. They ate it happily, and many persons still do.

Even so, the Central American armadillo prospered. By 1854 it had moved back as far north as southern Texas. Since then it has continued to spread eastward. Deserts have kept it from going very far to the west. And cold weather, as mentioned, has kept it from going north of Kansas and Missouri. But by the 1950s, armadillos had reached the Mississippi River. By the 1970s, they had crossed Mississippi and most of Alabama.

Today armadillos are living along the Atlantic Coast from South Carolina to the southern tip of Florida, and westward to New Mexico. However, most of those in Florida are not the result of this migration. About fifty years ago a number of armadillos escaped from a zoo in South Florida. They have been breeding and spreading northward ever since. Today in northern Florida they are mixing with those from the West.

In all this long migration how did the slow, heavily armored armadillo cross the creeks and rivers that barred its way? The answer is one of the strangest things about this strange animal.

Actually the armadillo has two methods of crossing water. Heavier than water, it may sink like a rock to the bottom. Then it can simply walk across, holding its breath for six or perhaps as long as ten minutes. Nobody knows exactly how long. But Dr. Storrs and her husband, Dr. Harry Burchfield, once chased an armadillo into a pond. There the armadillo went straight down. But the water was clear. From the bank the two scientists watched the animal walk along the bottom until it reached some underwater tree roots. Here, apparently, the armadillo thought it was safely hidden. And here it stayed for six minutes before it paddled to the surface, calmly climbed out—and was captured in a net.

On the other hand, an armadillo doesn't need to walk across the bottom of a pond or stream if it doesn't want to. Instead of blowing air out, the armadillo can take air in. It not only breathes in air to fill its lungs, it swallows air. It keeps swallowing until it is stuffed. Full of air, an armadillo may be three inches bigger around than it was before. Now it will float like an amphibious tank. Using its powerful, clawed feet and paddling furiously, it can row itself across a river.

Even so, just how armadillos crossed a river as broad as the Mississippi is uncertain. In a time of flood an armadillo may have caught hold of a floating log and drifted across. Possibly one wandered aboard a nighttime ferry. Or some may have crossed on bridges.

Bridges, of course, would be dangerous for an armadillo. It is probable that more persons have seen armadillos that were killed by automobiles than have seen the animals alive. Certainly some of these deaths have been caused by the armadillo's strange reflex action of jumping straight up when surprised. A slow-witted armadillo crossing a road may not be aware of an approaching automobile until it is very close. Often the auto might pass over the armadillo without touching it. But startled, the armadillo is likely to jump straight up. Then, even the armadillo's armor would not protect it.

4
THE ARMADILLO IN MEDICINE

Dr. Eleanor Storrs, who once watched an armadillo walk across the bottom of a pond, began her scientific study of this animal because of another of its strange traits.

Normally armadillos mate in summer and the young are born the following spring. They are born with their eyes open. At this time the armor is as soft as well-cured leather. But they mature rapidly. The armor toughens, and the young are able to look after themselves in a few months. However, they are not sexually mature until they are two years old.

None of that is particulary unusual. Dr. Storrs's interest lay in the fact that *female armadillos are the only mammals in all the world that regularly give birth to identical*

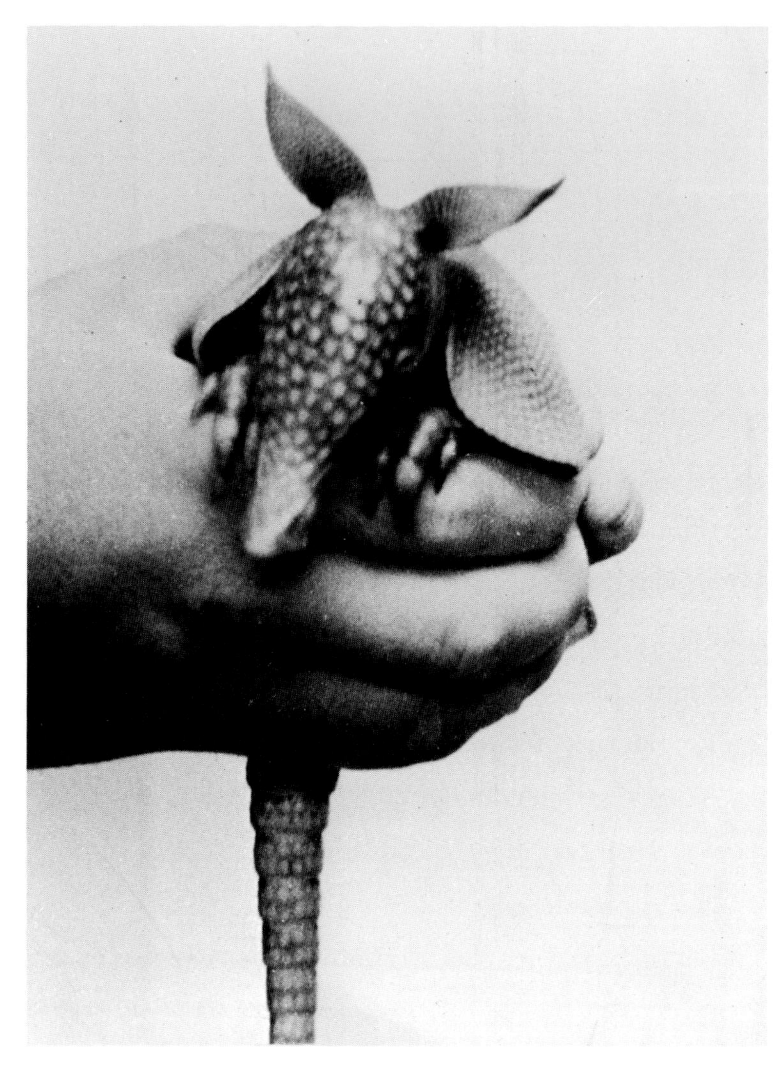

A baby nine-banded armadillo. The armor is soft when the armadillo is born.

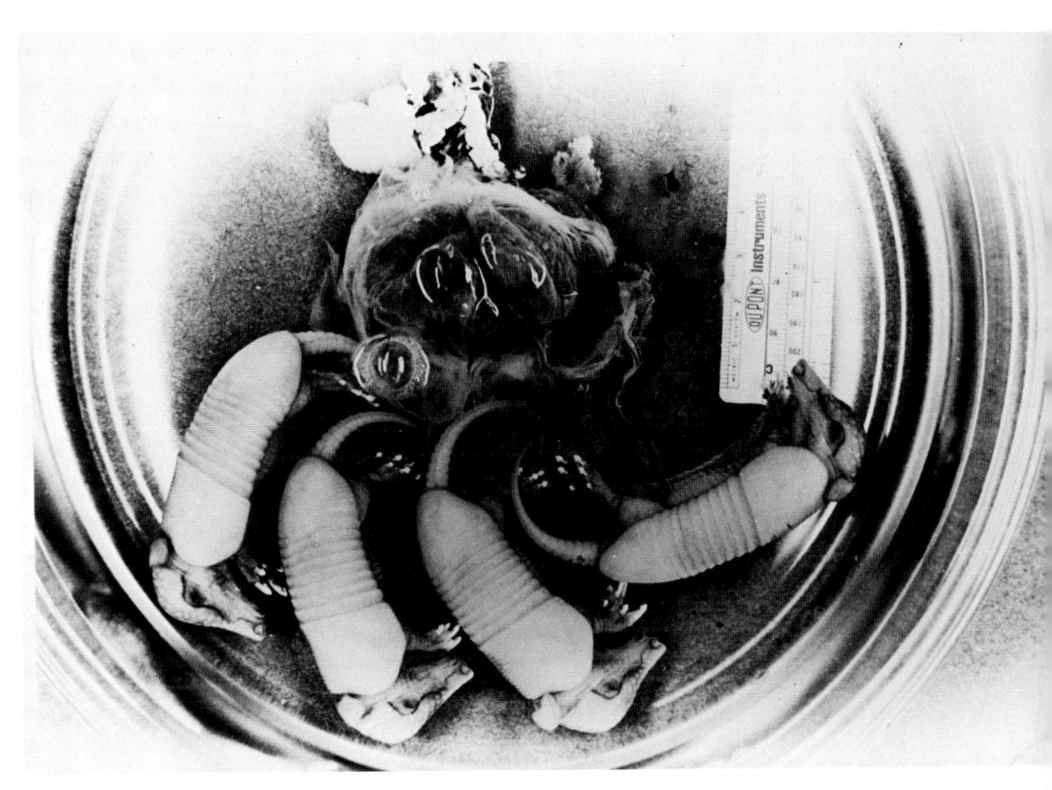

Quadruplet fetuses taken just before birth. A single embryo attaches to the mother's uterus, and shortly after buds to yield twins. Each twin buds again to produce quadruplets.

quadruplets. Not just sometimes, but practically always. Now and then one or two of the young may die before birth. Then the female will have triplets or twins. But under normal circumstances, the nine-banded armadillo

Three-month-old quadruplets

always has four pups, as the babies are called.

But that's not all. The four pups are identical, all coming from a single fertilized ovum, or egg, of the mother. Since all come from the same ovum, all have the same sets of genes. Genes are the microscopic units through which babies inherit characteristics of their parents. So the four pups of the armadillo should be absolutely identical, if the genes completely control inheritance. This was what Dr. Storrs set out to study.

South American Indians have a saying that, "Boy armadillos have no sisters, and girl armadillos have no brothers." Dr. Storrs soon learned that this was true, at least for any one set of pups. All four will be male, or all will be female. There are no mixed litters. Also, in most cases, the pups are carbon copies of one another, exactly alike. On the other hand, Dr. Storrs learned that differences do occur. Pups of the same litter sometimes differ physically much more than had been suspected.

As Pets

Dr. Storrs also learned, very early in her work, that armadillos make poor pets.

Since armadillos don't breed well in captivity, Dr. Storrs had to capture most of hers in the wild. Sometimes she was able to get a mother armadillo with young, but in captivity the mother would refuse to nurse her young. That meant the babies had to be hand fed. But often they refused to take food from a nipple or medicine dropper.

Then Dr. Storrs had to force-feed them with a stomach tube.

When big enough to feed themselves, the armadillos became almost too much at home. Like cats, they were easy to train to use a box of sand or torn paper as a toilet. But even so, they smelled. Like skunks, armadillos have scent glands near the tail. Fortunately, they don't have a true skunklike odor. But it is a musky odor, and any room where the armadillos stayed soon began to smell badly.

A hairy armadillo asleep at the Medical Research Center where Dr. Eleanor Storrs works. Hairy armadillos, unlike most, sleep on their backs.

Baby nine-banded armadillos. These were born at the Medical Research Center of Florida Technological University. These armadillos live in a concrete pen. Taken outside and placed on the ground, they instantly began to root for insects, although they had never been outside before.

During the day the armadillos were little trouble. They usually curled up in corners and slept. This left them fresh and ready to explore as soon as the lights went out at night.

Even when rooting through leaves and grass for food, an armadillo tends to be noisy. Across a wooden floor it goes bumping along like a truck without tires. It bangs into tables and chairs. It turns over things and goes crawling through the litter, pushing objects back and forth. If it finds itself in a corner, it is quite likely to spend the rest of the night trying to claw its way straight through the wall.

Dr. Storrs now has about three hundred armadillos. Many of them she knows by name, as you would a pet dog or cat. But she no longer keeps them in her home. Instead they are in pens in a large laboratory. It smells musky, but at night when the lights are out, there are no human beings close by trying to sleep.

Armadillos and Leprosy

While Dr. Storrs was studying armadillos, her husband, Dr. Harry Burchfield, was awarded a government grant for a different kind of research. He was to try to find a way to measure extremely small amounts of a drug used in treating persons who had leprosy.

Leprosy is one of the oldest and most feared of all human diseases. It was known long before Christ. From the eleventh through the thirteenth centuries it was widespread in Europe. It not only brought death, but also it might horribly disfigure its victims. Sometimes it caused blindness. Sometimes it caused the victim's nose or fingers or toes to rot away. But no one knew what caused it, or how it spread. In ancient Europe leprosy victims had to carry a rattle or bell, warning other persons not to come near.

By the late nineteenth century doctors were able to identify the bacterium that caused leprosy. But they did not know how to cure or prevent it. The leprosy bacteria would not grow in test tubes. Nor would they grow in any of the animals on which researchers experimented. Without a ready supply of these bacteria researchers could make little progress. And though leprosy is not as widespread as it once was, there are still more than 12 million cases in the world. Also, in recent years, the number of cases has once more been increasing.

This is why the World Health Organization and doctors around the world were trying so hard to find some kind of treatment.

It was well known that in its human victims leprosy attacked those parts of the body where the temperature is the lowest, such as the fingers and toes. A Dr. C.C. Shepard in Atlanta had been able to grow the leprosy bacteria in the cool footpads of a mouse. But this was in such small amounts as to be of little help.

When Dr. Eleanor Storrs learned this, she immediately thought of her armadillos. The normal temperature of these strange creatures is several degrees lower than that of most animals. In fact, where the average human temperature is 98.6° F (37° C), the temperature of an armadillo will range from 93° F (33° C) all the way down to 84° F (28° C).

Dr. Storrs's idea that armadillos might be able to have leprosy and so produce enough bacteria for study excited leprosy researchers around the world. A Dr. Chapman Binford of the Armed Forces Institute of Pathology in Washington, D.C., obtained diseased tissue from a leprosy victim in Surinam, South America. Doctors from a hospital in Carville, Louisiana, that treats leprosy victims came to help Dr. Storrs. And four armadillos were inoculated with the leprosy bacteria.

Seventeen months later, one of them died of leprosy.

The work on leprosy that now starts with Dr. Storrs's armadillos in Melbourne, Florida, goes on around the

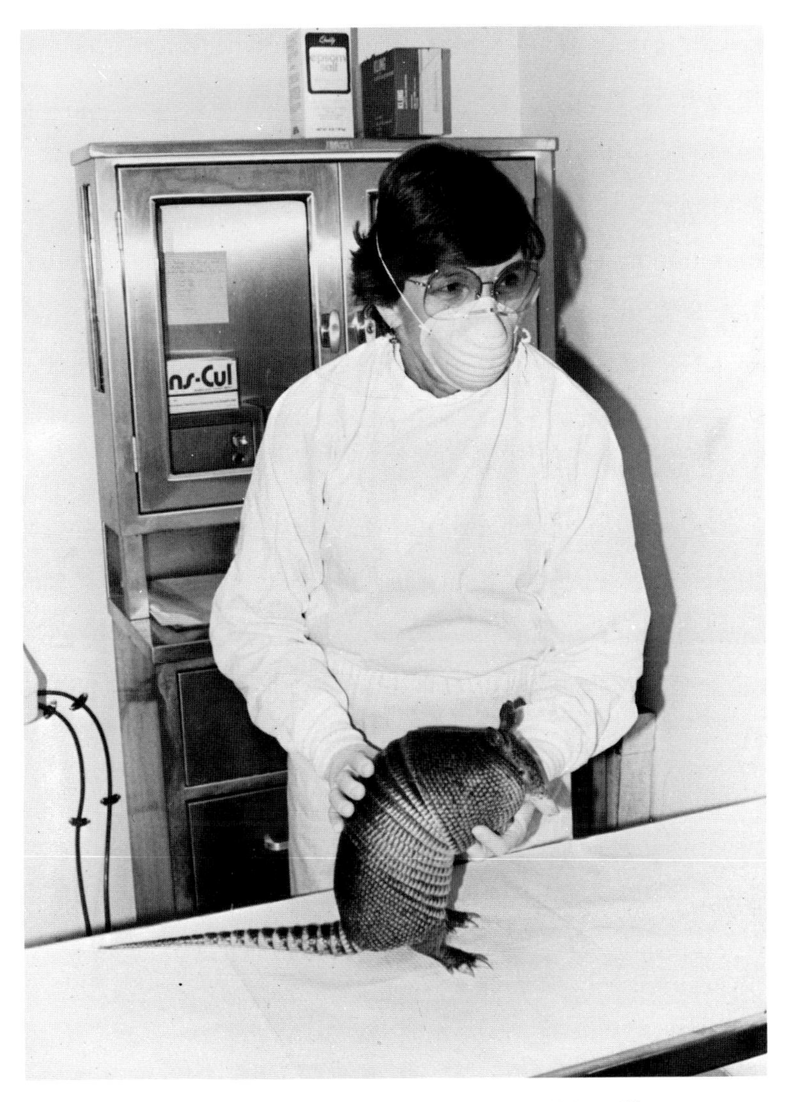

This is Dr. Eleanor Storrs with Katie, the armadillo TV star.

world. Tissue from the armadillos may be flown first to doctors in England where the bacterium is identified and purified. From there it may go to other doctors in Seattle, Washington, or Oslo, Norway, for study. Then back to London where scientists are working to develop a vaccine that will prevent leprosy. In Venezuela doctors already report some progress in the treatment of one of mankind's oldest and most horrible diseases.

All with the help of the strange little armadillo.

It is now known that in Louisiana a very few wild armadillos have leprosy. But whether they got it from one another, or from some contact with a human victim is not known. But doctors do not believe that any human being has ever gotten leprosy from an armadillo.

5
ARMADILLOS: IN T-SHIRTS, JEWELRY, AND RACES

The armadillo is a strange-looking animal, certainly. Very few persons would consider it beautiful, or even cute. Yet in Texas, which probably has more armadillos than any other state, the armadillo's figure has been used to make things both cute and beautiful. In fact, the armadillo has become a Texas symbol of both fashion and fun.

The armadillo fad may have started with cartoons in a humor magazine published at the University of Texas. These showed armadillos in humanlike poses, dancing, singing, sleeping. One was a picture of Rudolph the Red-nosed Armadillo leading Santa Claus's sled.

A newspaper reporter wrote a fanciful story about arma-

The armadillo may not be pretty, but in Texas it is popular. T-shirts, belt buckles, and many other items are made to feature the armadillo.

dillos predicting the weather the way groundhogs are said to do in the spring. He made up a yarn about hiding outside the armadillo's den to see if it would be frightened by its shadow. Another reporter made up a story about breeding armadillos for racing the way racehorses are bred.

And all at once there were armadillos everywhere. There were T-shirts with pictures of armadillos. There were armadillo toys, checkerboards with armadillo figures, shoes and hats made like armadillos. Soon there was armadillo jewelry: gold and silver rings, bracelets, pins shaped like armadillos. There were glass figurines of armadillos that cost as much as $500.

County fairs began to stage armadillo races. The armadillos are fast, but they are also dim-witted and not easy

A young Texan places his armadillo on the starting line ready for an armadillo race.

to train. The races had to be run down lanes with wire sides so the armadillos could not take off across country. Even so, one was as likely to run backward as forward.

The students of Oak Creek Elementary School in Houston, Texas, adopted the armadillo as the school mascot. They did research and wrote papers about it. They wrote to the Texas legislature saying that Texas had a state flower, the bluebonnet, and a state bird, the mockingbird. Now, they wrote, the legislature should adopt the armadillo as the "official state mammal."

It was all a lot of fun for the people—but not always for armadillos. Although their feet are tough for digging dens, they are easily cut by wire. Trying to escape from the wire-sided racetracks, they were often badly injured. Worse, as the fad spread, armadillos were killed by the thousands for their shells. These were made into banjos, baskets, flower vases, and other things.

People had always known that armadillos were eatable, much like good pork. But few people actually ate them. Then, almost suddenly, it became the fad to put armadillo meat in chili—and Texans eat a lot of chili. One company began to can and sell armadillo meat. It advertised it would pay $2.50 for any dead armadillo brought in. Some people began to kill them with rocks or guns or any way possible. The Humane Society of the United States objected. The Texas Health Department closed one meat company because it used spoiled armadillo meat. Laws protecting the armadillo are now being considered.

The armadillo benefits man by helping find a treatment for leprosy. Man doesn't always help the armadillo in return. But the strange little creature has been around for several million years. It will probably be around for a long time in the future.

6
SOME OTHER ARMADILLOS AND RELATIVES

There are about twenty species of armadillos, but scientists now know very little about some of them. All, except *Dasypus novemcinctus*, the nine-banded armadillo, are confined to Central and South America. Much study still needs to be done.

The smallest of all the armadillos is called *Chlamyphorus truncatus*. At least it is called that by any scientist who can pronounce it. It is also called the lesser pichiciago. Or it might be called the twenty-two-banded armadillo, since its tiny body is covered by twenty-two movable bands of armor.

But the very few persons who have ever seen *Chlamy-*

The least armadillo is also called the fairy armadillo. It lives in western Argentina and is very rare. This is a picture of a mounted specimen in the Smithsonian.

phorus truncatus usually call it the least, or the fairy, armadillo. It is only about eight inches long, including the tail. The tiny bands of armor are pale pink. They cover only part of the armadillo's sides; the rest of the body and the legs are a mass of soft white hair.

This tiny and rare armadillo is found nowhere except western Argentina. Like most of its relatives it lives in a den, often with long tunnels leading to the main room. Normally it only comes out at night, which is one reason so few persons have ever seen it. Frightened, it can dig swiftly into the ground. Since it is only a few inches long it doesn't take much of a hole to crawl into. And once in the hole it has an added protection against most enemies: the rear end of the fairy armadillo is a solid plate of armor. With its short tail tucked under its belly, this solid plate serves as a stopper to the armadillo's hole.

Photograph of a mounted specimen— the giant armadillo.

The fairy armadillo has a close relative called *Burmeisteria retusa*, or the greater pichiciago. Actually it is only a few inches bigger than the fairy, or lesser pichiciago. Its armor covers a little more of its sides. It too is found in western Argentina and in Bolivia.

In contrast to the eight-inch fairy armadillo, there is the giant armadillo of Brazil. Scientifically it is called *Priodontes maximus* or sometimes *Priodontes giganteus.* It may be as much as forty inches long, not counting the tail, and may weigh up to 120 pounds. It may have eleven, twelve, or even thirteen bands of armor and these are black on the back and grayish on the sides. Like the nine-banded armadillo, it can stand on its hind legs, using its tail as a prop. Since it needs a big den, it has very long, strong claws. In fact, the third finger claws may measure seven inches along the curve.

Despite its size, the giant armadillo is as timid as its smaller relatives. Frightened, it tries to find a hole in which to hide. If it can't find a hole, it tries to roll into a ball. Unfortunately, its shell isn't big enough to cover its whole body.

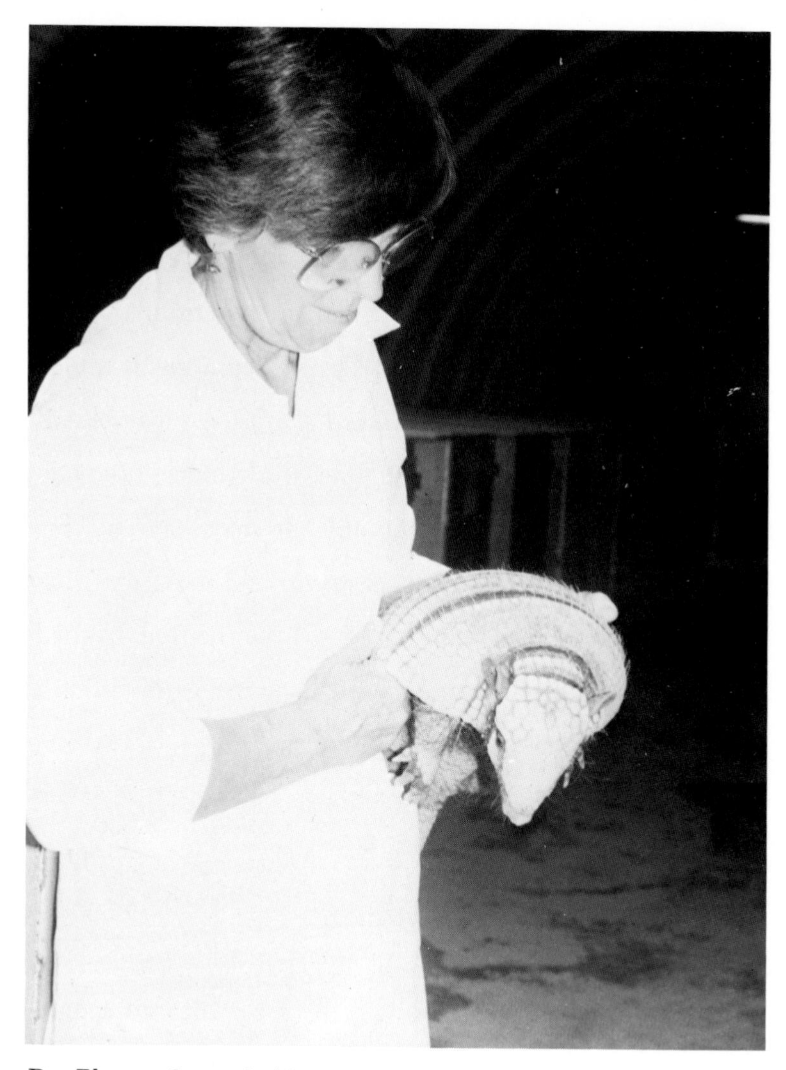

Dr. Eleanor Storrs holding an adult six-banded armadillo. These are larger than the nine banded, this one weighing twenty pounds.

Many persons believe that all armadillos can roll into balls, the armor covering the entire body. Actually only the three-banded armadillo can do this. Scientifically there are two species of the three-banded armadillo, *Tolypeutes matacus* and *Tolypeutes tricinctus*, but there is not enough difference for most persons to worry about. The three bands are fairly narrow; the solid armor over the shoulders and hips is wide. These can be swung together, almost like the sides of a clam shell, with the armored head and tail closing the gaps.

The hairy armadillo, *Chaetophractus villosus*, is not

A hairy armadillo in Brazil

The soft-tailed armadillo from Brazil

likely to win any beauty prizes, even among armadillos. Much like its nine-banded relative in many ways, maybe a little bigger, it gets its name from the stiff, bristlelike hairs that grow between its bands and cover its belly. Its bands come down low on its sides. In danger, if it can't find a place to hide, it will double up its legs and lower its armor to touch the ground. It may also make a snarling noise, but that's just bluff.

Strangely, the hairy armadillo likes to sleep on its back, all four legs in the air. It lives in Argentina and in Uruguay.

Sloths

The modern word "slow" comes from the Old English word "slǣwth," meaning slow. The word "sloth" comes from the same source, but sloth means more than just slow, it means lazy and not wanting to move or work. So when English-speaking people first saw an animal that hung belly-up from tree limbs, looked more like a clump of leaves than an animal, and moved very, very slowly when it moved at all, they called it a sloth.

Sloths live in the forests of Central and South America.

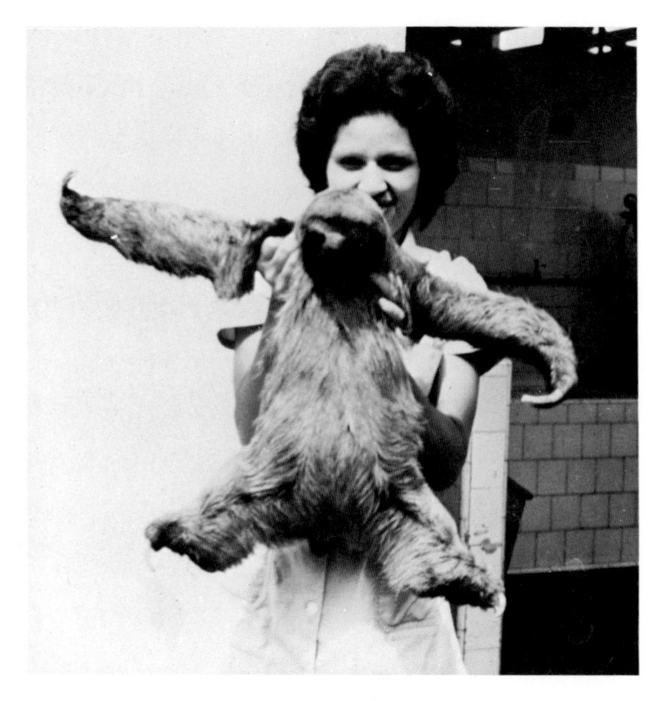

A three-toed sloth in Rio de Janeiro. This one lived as a pet, moving freely, but very slowly, about the trees in a large garden.

They spend almost their entire lives hanging from tree limbs, almost never coming to the ground. They feed on leaves and fruit. These are plentiful and don't run away, so there is no need for a sloth to hurry. Its top speed, if it really rushes along a branch, is about thirteen feet a minute. If under some extreme condition it has to leave one tree in order to move to another, it can make only about six feet a minute on the ground. Here it would be an easy prey for a jaguar or some other large animal. But the sloth rarely travels on the ground. It not only eats and sleeps hanging belly-up from tree limbs, it mates and gives birth in this position.

There are actually two genera of tree sloths, the three-toed, *Bradypus tridactylus*, and the two-toed sloth, *Choloepus hoffmanni.* The names explain the main difference between them: the two-toed sloths have two toes on their front feet, three on the back; the three-toed sloths have three toes all around. Both are about twenty-seven inches long with long, rough hair of a brownish color. But the sloth moves so slowly hanging from its tree limbs in rain or sun, that algae grow on its hairs much as they do on the tree limbs, and this may affect the color.

Anteaters

The anteaters of Central and South America, along with the tree sloths, are the only relatives of the armadillo. And

A giant anteater—a mounted display in the Smithsonian

if armadillos and sloths are strange creatures, so are their anteater cousins.

By far the most impressive of the anteaters is the giant anteater *Myrmecophaga tridactyla.* It's a full seven feet long, if you count three feet of tail. This tail is as bushy as an Indian's warbonnet and looks even longer than it is. At the other end of the anteater is a long head, most of which is a pipelike, down-sloping muzzle. Back of the head is a long, heavy neck. Between the neck and tail there is a short, heavy body. The whole thing can weigh one hundred pounds or more.

And it lives on nothing but ants and termites. It almost has to, considering the shape of the long, slender muzzle and small mouth. Like the armadillo, its teeth are no good for biting or chewing. But it has wonderful weapons to use against ants and termites. Its toes are tipped by powerful claws for tearing open the homes of its prey. And inside its narrow muzzle is a tongue sixteen inches long, coated with a thick saliva. Plunged into an ant or termite hill, this comes back coated with insects. If the ants sting, it doesn't seem to bother the anteater. It just keeps eating.

Anteaters lead lonely lives except during the mating season. One baby is born at a time, and this rides around on its mother's back for about three months, then goes off on its own. During its time with the mother, it is taught how to feed on ants and termites.

And here is one of the strangest things about these

strange Xenarthra animals. In the wild an anteater eats nothing but ants and termites. But a baby anteater born in a zoo and brought up without its mother won't touch either one!

The lesser anteater, *Tamandua longicaudata*, is usually just called the tamandua. It is only about half the size of the giant anteater. Like its big relative it feeds on ants and termites, but it hunts for them chiefly in trees. It does not have the huge, bushy tail of the giant; living in trees so much of the time such a tail would be a handicap. Instead tamandua has a monkeylike tail it can use in climbing.

When tamandua comes down to earth to rest between meals, it doesn't have to depend on its claws for protection. It also has a skunklike weapon; it can give off an odor that sends other animals galloping away. Mother tamanduas often use this to protect their young.

The smallest member of the anteater family is the two-toed anteater, *Cyclopes didactylus*. It is only about sixteen inches long. Like tamandua, it hunts its food in trees, eating bees as well as ants and termites. Actually, the two-toed anteater has five toes on its hind feet and four on its

A mounted display of the tamandua

front feet. But only two of the four front toes have claws.

Like other anteaters, the two-toed lives mostly alone. It hunts at night. Naturalists in the future will need to study it because very little is now known.

In fact, there is still much for scientists to learn about all these strange anteaters, sloths, and armadillos.

INDEX